HONEY, I
shrunk
THE KIDS

A novel by B.B. Hiller and Neil W. Hiller
based on the motion picture from
Walt Disney Pictures
produced by Penny Finkelman Cox
based on the screenplay by
Ed Naha and Tom Schulman and
story by
Stuart Gordon, Brian Yuzna and Ed Naha
directed by Joe Johnston

Hippo Books
Scholastic Children's Books
London

Scholastic Children's Books,
Scholastic Publications Ltd.,
7-9 Pratt Street, London NW1 0AE

Scholastic Inc.,
730 Broadway, New York, NY 10003, USA

Scholastic Canada Ltd.,
123 Newkirk Road, Richmond Hill,
Ontario, Canada L4C 3G5

Ashton Scholastic Pty Ltd.,
PO Box 579, Gosford, New South Wales,
Australia

Ashton Scholastic Ltd.,
Private Bag 1, Penrose, Auckland,
New Zealand

First published by Scholastic Inc., New York, 1989
Published in the UK by Scholastic Publications Ltd, 1990

Copyright © Walt Disney, 1990

ISBN 0 590 76306 7

Made and printed by Cox & Wyman Ltd, Reading, Berks
Typeset by AKM Associates (UK) Ltd, Southall, London

10 9 8 7 6 5 4 3 2

For Michael J. Sarg, Jr, M.D.

CONTENTS

1

SATURDAY MORNING

It was a warm and sunny Saturday morning. In the neat and tidy back garden of the Thompsons' house, ten-year-old Ron Thompson was noisily pitching a tent. Ron was a Cub Scout. His fifteen-year-old brother, Little Russ, was lifting weights nearby. Their father, Big Russ, called weight lifting pumping iron. Big Russ worked for the Olympian Construction Company.

Suddenly, a window on the first floor of the Thompsons' house whooshed open. Big Russ leaned out on the windowsill and stuck his head and shoulders out. Even though he'd just got up and was still in rumpled pyjamas, Mr Thompson already wore his favourite hat, a Giants baseball cap, pulled down low on his head. He glared at his watch and then down at the kids.

"What are you two doing?" he yelled. "And at this hour?"

Ron continued hammering away. He called to Big Russ without looking up at him, "Pitching a tent, Dad."

"Don't you know I'm sleeping?"

"But you're *talking* to us, Dad." Ron looked up at the window. "You look wide awake."

Ron smiled innocently at his father. Big Russ glared back, then withdrew his head and slammed the bedroom window shut.

Ron slumped to the ground with a disappointed look on his face.

"What's wrong, Ron?" his brother asked.

"This," Ron waved at the tent, "is sissy stuff."

"What is?"

"Camping in the yard. I want to camp out in the real jungle. With wild animals. Cannibals. Grizzly bears. . . ."

Little Russ made a sour face at Ron. "Grizzly bears don't live in the jungle," he said.

"They do in *my* jungle. And they'd eat kids like you for breakfast."

Ron liked to tease his brother as much as he liked to upset their father.

Little did either of them know that Ron was going to get his wish for a wild jungle. And soon.

2

THE AMAZING PULSE DEVICE

Amy Szalinski was watching the Thompson boys that sunny Saturday morning. She studied them, mostly Little Russ, from the kitchen window of the rundown Szalinski house next door to the Thompson house.

Amy sighed. Like Little Russ, she was fifteen. But she was tall, rather than short like Russ. And she wore glasses. Russ just didn't seem to notice her. She sighed again and returned to making breakfast for the rest of her family.

Amy's mother had had an argument with Amy's father the night before, and her mother had spent the night at Amy's grandmother's house. Amy was filling in for her mum as best she could.

But cooking wasn't one of Amy's strong points.

She picked up the bowl of eggs she had just finished beating and looked down at her nine-year-old brother, Nick. He was seated across the table, reading a science fiction paperback, as usual. Amy put some bread in the toaster near

Nick. "Watch the toast for me, Nick," Amy said.

"Sure," Nick said without looking up from his paperback. The book he was absorbed in that morning was called *Peace Feelers and Other Stories*. Amy noticed that Nick's current book had the sort of weird creature cover Nick seemed to prefer for light reading. Nick was small and thin, and seemed to be allergic to everything. He was not much help around the house.

Amy walked to the sink and ran cold water into the bowl of eggs. Then she crossed the kitchen to the stove and poured the mixture of eggs and water into a waiting frying pan. She turned the flame down to low heat. Nick laid his book down and walked over to the stove. On his tiptoes, he peered into the pan.

"Mum never made scrambled eggs that looked like *that*," Nick said, gazing back and forth from the eggs up to Amy's face.

"Mum's not here."

"When do you think she's coming back?" Nick asked, glancing at the eggs suspiciously again.

"I don't know. Maybe never. . . ." Amy said.

"I hope she comes back soon," Nick replied.

"How is the toast coming?" his sister asked.

"Fine," Nick told her, without looking at the toaster.

4

"Then how come it's smoking?"

Nick strolled back to the table and sat down. "It's hot?" he asked brightly. He pulled up the toaster handle. Two smoking black squares rose slowly into view.

Amy walked to the table holding the frying pan and scraped some of its contents onto the plate in front of Nick. "A straight-A student, but you can't make toast," Amy complained.

"I want to be a scientist like Dad. Not a cook," Nick told her.

"Where is Dad?" Amy asked him.

"Upstairs," Nick told her.

"As usual."

At that moment, Wayne Szalinski, physicist, was tinkering with his latest invention in his attic "laboratory". Amy and Nick's dad wore one red sock and one yellow, with rumpled clothing above. He chattered happily to Quark, the family terrier, about his "electromagnetic pulse invention."

It looked like a very big amateur radio station.

Puzzled, Quark listened to Mr Szalinski. Quark had been named after a mysterious subatomic particle.

"This is it, Quark. A red-letter day." Mr Szalinski flicked a switch. The machine began to

5

hum. Quark retreated towards the door.

"A common laser device, you say?" asked Mr Szalinski. Quark's ears flopped up. "Wrong, Quark. It's an *amazing* electromagnetic pulse device. If this honey works and my calculations are correct, its computer scanners will home in on a solid object, analyse and isolate its molecular structure, and then reduce the space between its electrons. You know what that means, don't you?"

Quark just stared at his master.

"It will actually *shrink* the object. It will be a real boon to the space programme and other scientific work."

Quark yawned. Mr Szalinski took an apple from a paper bag on the couch. Quark barked and wagged his tail. Maybe it was snack time! Quark carefully approached the strange equipment. To Quark's disappointment, his master walked over to a large steel plate and placed the apple on a pedestal in front of the plate.

Quark retreated to the door.

Mr Szalinski put on a set of safety goggles. He walked across the attic to Quark's place by the door and absent-mindedly put another set of goggles on the dog. The scientist walked back across the attic to his strange machine.

"The only problem is that I haven't got this thing to work yet. But I'm close, Quark. I'm very, very close."

Mr Szalinski activated his double-beamed machine. The beams crackled in the air. They joined to form a powerful single beam which was focused on the apple. A shimmer of light shone around the apple. It began to vibrate in the glare.

Suddenly, the apple exploded in a powerful spray of warm apple sauce.

Dejectedly, Mr Szalinski flicked off the machine. Its beams died and its vibrations wound down. The scientist stripped off his goggles and flopped on to the couch. "A bummer, Quark," he grunted. Quark trotted over and jumped up on to the couch. He began to lick the apple sauce off his master's face. Mr Szalinski scribbled something on a large mound of notes stacked on the couch next to him.

The scientist brightened and looked up from his notes. He said to Quark with a smile, "On the plus side, we have discovered a very expensive way to make apple sauce!"

A SHATTERING EXPERIENCE

At the kitchen table, Mr Szalinski picked at the watery yellow stuff on his breakfast plate with a pencil. "Umm. Looks *interesting*." He glanced up at Amy. "What is it?"

Amy looked embarrassed. "Scrambled eggs," she told her dad.

Her father made a note on his stack of papers. They were now next to his plate. He absent-mindedly picked up a fork and attempted to get some of the egg to stay on it. The egg ran through the fork and back on to his plate. He looked up at his daughter again.

"I'll get you a spoon," she said, rising from the table.

Mr Szalinski picked up a piece of charred toast and stared at it curiously. Nick announced, "I'm allergic to eggs." Then, just to be on the safe side, Nick added, "I'm also allergic to toast."

Amy paused thoughtfully at the silverware drawer across the kitchen. "Did you pick up Nick's allergy pills, Dad?"

Her father was busy scribbling notes. He seemed not to hear her.

"I suppose you also forgot my dress from the cleaners?" Amy asked.

Mr Szalinski continued to scribble.

Amy was upset. "Dad. How *could* you? I need that dress for the school dance on Friday night."

"Nobody's asked you to go," Nick reminded her unnecessarily.

Nick poured himself a bowl of Cornflakes from the box that was always on the kitchen table.

"No wonder Mum left us," Amy said. "All you ever think about is that shrinking machine, Dad."

Her father looked up from his notes at last. "It's an *amazing* electromagnetic pulse device," he said.

The phone rang in the hallway. Mr Szalinski jumped up, gathered his notes, and ran out of the room to answer it.

Amy walked over to Nick and lifted the plate of eggs from his place. "If you don't want this wholesome food," she declared, "Quark will eat it." She dumped the contents of the plate into Quark's bowl on the floor.

The family terrier ambled over and sniffed at his bowl. He looked up at Amy and cocked his head curiously at her. Then he backed away from

9

the bowl and lay down. He put his chin on his paws and closed his eyes.

A little while later, Mr Szalinski stepped outside the front door. He was leaving for the Scientific Congress to present his paper on his amazing machine. His rumpled notepapers were now in a battered briefcase under his arm. Nick and Amy chorused, "Good luck, Dad," before the door clicked closed behind him.

Then they counted to three together. The door popped open and their father stuck his head in.

"Wish me luck, kids." He smiled at them.

"Good luck, Dad," they said again.

"I'll be back in a few hours," said their father.

Mr Szalinski walked towards his car at the kerb. Big Russ, in his Giants cap, leaned over the fence between the Thompson and Szalinski back gardens. Mrs Thompson was nearby working on her pride and joy, her flower beds.

"Hey, Szalinski," Big Russ said, "I was thinking that you might fix up your garden one of these days. It's beginning to look like a jungle."

"Taken care of," Amy's father answered proudly. "I hired Tommy Pervis to cut the grass."

"Your house could do with sprucing up, too," Big Russ went on.

10

"Russ!" Mrs Thompson exclaimed in shock, looking up from a nearby petunia patch.

"Tell you what, Russ, maybe I'll hire Olympian Construction to do the job," Mr Szalinski offered.

"No way . . ." Russ began.

Amy's father got into his car, started it, and drove off.

Mrs Thompson chuckled, rose, and wandered off to the back garden.

"Egghead," Big Russ muttered. He pulled his hat from his head and reached for a cigarette he had hidden inside it.

"You're not thinking of having a cigarette, are you, Russ?" Mrs Thompson sang from the back garden. She was having a hard time getting Big Russ to stop smoking.

Russ jammed the hat back on his head.

In the Thompson back garden, Ron was trying to figure out how to have some fun.

"You're not going to try and shave Cicero again, are you?" Little Russ asked Ron. Cicero was the Thompson family cat. He watched the twins from a safe and wary distance at the edge of their yard.

"No," Ron began, "better than that. Come on."

Ron had something hidden behind his back.

11

The boys now stood near the fence separating the Thompson and Szalinski back gardens. When Mrs Thompson returned to the front garden, Ron produced a bottle of maple syrup.

"Does Mum know you have that?" Little Russ asked.

Ron poured syrup on to the top of the fence. Flies began to land in it. The insects were instantly trapped in the goo, and Ron's face was gleeful. "Gotcha," he told a hapless fly.

"Yuk," Little Russ said with distaste. "Hey, here comes Dad. He looks really angry."

"Dad's *always* angry," Ron replied, "even when he's happy." He pitched the open bottle over the fence into the Szalinski back garden. There the syrup bottle drained slowly on to the ground.

"What are you two up to?" Big Russ demanded as he approached them.

"Why, nothing, Dad," Ron answered. "We're just watching bugs."

"Well," Big Russ said. "Make sure you watch *our* bugs and not the ones in the Szalinski garden." With that, he turned to Little Russ, who was still working out with his weights. "Better get a move on, Son. You're going to be late for football practice."

"Dad, I'm not on the team any more. I've been cut," Little Russ said in a rush. It was hard to talk with his dad.

"You've got to get out there to get an edge on the other boys," his father said. He hadn't listened to a word Little Russ had said to him.

"Dad," Little Russ said more loudly and slowly. "Dad, I'm not on the team any more. Coach Farrell cut me from the roster. He said I was too small and too light for football. He said I should try ballet."

Big Russ narrowed his eyes. "Bernie Farrell did that to me, huh? Well, we played baseball together, and I used to knock him down whenever I felt like it." He hitched up his shorts, pulled down his cap brim, and lifted his chin. "Ballet, huh? Maybe I ought to go and knock him down a few more times as a reminder of whose son you are. Too small and too light my —"

"*Dad,*" Little Russ pleaded, "it's all right . . . *please.* . . ." Little Russ watched sadly as his father stalked off.

His mum walked over. "Looks like you finally told him."

"Yeah, I told him," Little Russ said sadly. "I really told him."

* * *

13

In another part of the garden Ron had picked up a baseball and bat.

Nick sat in the kitchen window of the house next door, building a Lego castle on the sill. It was the window his sister Amy had gazed out of earlier in the morning. "Better watch out," Nick called to Ron. "You might hit the beehive in that tree." Nick pointed with a piece of his castle before snapping it into place.

"What do *you* know about baseball, baby egghead?" Ron yelled.

"I know about bees," Nick called back. "Bees can kill you if you're allergic and *I'm* allergic." He hurriedly closed the window. Some of his Lego pieces were knocked off the windowsill and fell to the ground below in the process.

Ron pulled the bat back and swung. He connected solidly with the ball. The familiar sound of wood on leather echoed across the yard as a hard-hit line drive shot from the bat.

It shattered the Szalinski attic window.

4

IT WORKS!

The baseball was perched shakily on a small metal plate above the central workings of Mr Szalinski's machine. The ball tottered, then fell into the machine. There, among the jumble of parts and tangle of wires, it wedged firmly.

The baseball was blocking the power pack of one of the machine's two particle beam cannons. The workings of the machine were controlled by a powerful computer.

Suddenly, the machine came to life. The computer screen flicked on.

Then the machine went berserk.

The two beam cannons were unsteady as they scanned the attic workshop for targets. The one blocked by the baseball didn't work at all.

Suddenly, the couch Mr Szalinski liked to sit on, his "thinking couch," appeared on the screen. An intensely bright white beam shot from the working cannon. There was a loud pop!

The couch disappeared from the computer screen — and from the attic.

Or so it seemed.

The nearby armchair appeared on the screen and similarly disappeared with another pop and flash of light.

The armchair was followed by a trunk. Then almost everything else in the attic. In fact, the only things not to disappear were the glass from the broken window and the splatters of apple sauce.

The machine continued to scan the otherwise empty attic. It turned on its long range scanners. A view of the attic stairs appeared on the screen. . . .

Amy and Nick stood in the Szalinski back garden near the fence. Ron stood behind Little Russ, who was speaking.

"We'll get the window fixed, somehow," he said. He glanced over his shoulder and frowned. He turned back to Amy and Nick. "We'll pay for it out of Ron's allowance," he told his neighbours.

"But I didn't *do* anything," Ron complained.

Ron peered past Russ to look at Amy. "Can we at least get our ball back?" he asked. "Puleeeeze?"

"Oh, all right," Amy agreed. "Nick, take him up to the attic and give him back his ball." Ron clambered over the fence and trailed Nick into the Szalinski house.

"I'm really sorry. . ." Russ began.

"You should be," Amy told him.

Russ paused, tried again. "Uh, I saw you throwing the Frisbee to Quark yesterday. You're pretty good."

Amy was surprised by Russ's compliment. "Thank you," she said.

"Have you ever played sports with other people?" Russ asked.

The computer screen showed the two younger kids coming up the attic stairs.

"Wow! Look at this stuff," Ron exclaimed as the boys opened the upper attic door and walked into Mr Szalinski's laboratory. "It's right out of *Star Trek*!"

"It's my dad's stuff," Nick told him casually. "He works for an aerospace company."

Ron looked in the attic's corners for the ball. The room appeared to be completely empty. He turned to Nick. "Your dad's a mad scientist?" Ron asked.

Nick paused to consider it. "No, most of the time Dad seems to be pretty calm."

Ron stepped on something that crunched. He

stooped down to pick up a tiny trunk from the floor. "Hey," he said, holding the "trunk" out to Nick. "This looks like a free gift from a Cornflakes packet, only better."

Nick ignored Ron. The machine didn't. Ron's image appeared on the screen.

"Hey," Nick finally realized what he felt was wrong about the laboratory. "All my mum's furniture is gone!"

Nick turned in time to see a beam focused on Ron. Then Ron disappeared with a loud bang and a brillant flash of light. Nick was thrown to the floor by the force of the beam. As the laser cannon dropped to aim at him on the floor, Nick crawled to the spot where Ron had last stood. There, on the floor, as small as could be, was Ron waving up at him excitedly.

"It works!" Nick said. Then he saw that the machine was pointing at him. The laser cannon flashed. Nick disappeared with an explosive pop and a blaze of white light.

In the yard, Amy and Russ grew restless from waiting. "Do you like basketball?" Russ asked, looking up into Amy's face.

"Do you like *short* stories?" Amy responded, looking down into Russ's face.

18

Tommy Pervis arrived at that moment. He began preparing the power mower to cut the Szalinski lawn. He also seemed intent on finishing his usual brown bag full of cookies.

"If you see your dad, Amy, please tell him I'll have to start a little later on the lawn. My mum is going to pick me up any minute. I have to get some new trainers at the mall."

Amy nodded to Tommy, then she told Russ, "I'm going upstairs. Your brother better not be teasing my brother." She turned to go. Russ hopped over the fence and followed her.

As Amy went through the door into her father's laboratory, the machine zapped her with a great crash and flash. She vanished.

Russ's image replaced Amy's on the computer screen.

Just in time, Russ spotted the particle beam gun aimed at him. He dived for the floor as the machine's first shot at him sailed past his head with a loud bang and crash. Russ zigzagged as he wriggled across the floor on his elbows towards the attic door.

The crawling figure was in focus on the computer screen. A close-up of the small of his back replaced the full length shot on the screen. The cannon fired and Russ disappeared, too.

A scorched baseball popped out of the machine and rolled across the attic floor and into the far corner of the room. The machine shut down, its lights and screen fading. Seeming to sigh, it whined to a shuddering halt with a final, loud click.

5

BAGGED

Russ got to his feet slowly, dusting himself off.

He turned to Nick, who was standing nearby.

"What happened? Where are we?" Russ asked.

The two boys gazed upwards. They seemed to be in some gigantic cathedral with a mile-high ceiling. Amy and Ron looked on from behind Nick.

"We haven't *gone* anywhere," Nick answered. "We're still here in the attic. We've just been shrunk, that's all."

"Oh, good," Russ frowned at Nick. "Just shrunk."

Amy stomped up to Russ. "Why didn't you go for help?" she asked him.

"How was I to know what was going on up here?" Russ replied. "*You* didn't."

"You could have moved faster. Ducked the beam," Amy told Russ.

"Yeah," Russ said. "Just the way all the rest of you did. What do we do now?"

"I guess we wait until Dad gets home," Amy said. "He'll know what to do."

Russ and Ron exchanged knowing looks with each other.

They heard Quark barking downstairs. "Amy . . . Nick . . . I'm home," Mr Szalinski called from below.

"It's *Dad*!" Nick exclaimed.

The four youngsters began to yell as loudly as they could. But their voices were now as small as their quarter-inch-tall bodies.

"Kids?" Mr Szalinski called again. "I'm home. Amy? Nick?"

The kids heard the downstairs door to the attic open. A giant's thunderous footsteps pounded up the stairs. The door to the laboratory crashed open and closed. The floorboards shook as the giant strode across the room. He was followed by an excited Quark, sniffing his way across the attic floor suspiciously.

"Dad!" Amy screamed. "We're down here."

"Mr Szalinski!" Russ yelled.

"Hey, egghead!" Ron shouted.

Mr Szalinski noticed the pieces of broken glass. They were lying on top of the machine and scattered around it on the floor. The pieces of glass upset him.

"What else can go wrong?" he wondered out loud to Quark and to the world in general. "The Scientific Congress was a complete disaster. They didn't even like my *tie*, let alone my amazing invention." He glanced at the machine. "I don't know why, Quark, even you can see it's a perfectly good tie."

Mr Szalinski sat down without looking at the place where his thinking couch usually stood. But the couch was not there. He fell clumsily to the floor with a heavy thud. The floor shook when he landed. The shrunken children were rattled by the tremors of the crash. Mr Szalinski staggered back to his feet and thumped out of the attic and down the stairs.

In the first floor hallway, Amy's father phoned Amy's mother at his mother-in-law's. She wasn't there. At the beep of the answering machine, he spoke, "This is your husband, Wayne. I don't mind you taking your furniture from the attic when I'm not home. But the couch? My *thinking* couch? And where are the kids? I'd appreciate you returning them when you've done with them." He slammed the phone down.

Quark sat at the foot of the attic stairs and whined.

"Nobody likes a whiner, Quark," Mr Szalinski

told him. He reached out and scratched behind the dog's ears. "Except me."

A few minutes later, Mr Szalinski climbed the stairs to the attic. Again, the noise of his arrival was deafening to the kids. Again they tried to yell for his attention. This time he was carrying a broom, a dustpan, and the kitchen rubbish bin. He began to sweep up the broken glass from the floor.

Suddenly, Russ realized what was about to happen. "Scatter," Russ ordered. But it was too late.

The youngsters were swept into the dustpan.

Then they were dumped into the kitchen rubbish bag.

After a long wait, as the dust and junk from the floor was emptied on top of them, Mr Szalinski sealed the bag with its drawstring and lifted it from the kitchen container.

The kids were in near-total darkness. They were also being tossed all over the place with each step Mr Szalinski took. He carried the bag, swaying from its drawstring, downstairs out of the house and into the back garden.

He dropped it on the ground with a thump next to the rest of the rubbish at the back of the Szalinski's garden.

6

MOWER POWER TO YOU

Tiny voices came from the rubbish bag leaning against the rear fence of the Szalinski's garden. One was Ron's.

"What is this sludge? More of your father's experiments?"

"They're *eggs*," Amy insisted.

"From what kind of bird?" Ron asked her.

"Oh, forget it," Amy replied, leaping to a carbonized toast island to get her wet ankles out of the eggs.

"Lion Scouts to the rescue!" Ron yelled. He felt his way to the side of the bag and cut a large slit in it with a broken piece of glass. Then Ron stuck his foot through the slit and sat down.

Whooping all the way, Ron "rode" the slit in the bag to the ground.

He tore the bag wide open as he went. Don, Russ, Amy, and Nick emerged from the bag a moment later, blinking in the daylight after the darkness in the bag.

The kids turned to face their new world.

It was awesome.

The back garden was transformed into an alien landscape. Blades of grass looked like a redwood forest. Their tips could not be seen from the ground. Only a little of the sunlight filtered through the grass and actually reached the ground where the kids stood among the "trunks" of the grass. Constant noise struck the kids' ears: crackling, buzzing, chomping noise. The jungle in the back garden was alive!

"Our only hope is to get back to the house," Amy said. "If Dad's 'amazing pulse device' can shrink us, it can enlarge us, too. Right, Nick?"

Nick answered uneasily. "I *suppose* he could reverse the process," he said.

"All right," Amy said. "Then all we have to do" — she gazed up at the mountain-sized house which seemed a thousand miles away — "is get across the yard."

Nick also stared at the vast distance to the house. He began to cough. Then he sneezed. He pulled out a tissue and dabbed at his face.

Russ turned to Amy. "What's his problem?" he asked.

"He's allergic," Amy told him.

"To what?" Russ asked.

"To life," Ron volunteered.

"Look," Amy began, "maybe you and your brother had better get back to the house on your own. My brother and I may have to stay here. I don't know if Nick can make it that far."

"That doesn't sound very —" Russ began.

"The beanpole's right," Ron said. He was talking about Amy. "The wimpoid," Ron meant Nick, "will just slow the rest of us down."

Amy turned on Ron fiercely. Shut it, motor-mouth," she told him.

"I hate girls who are bigger than me," Ron muttered.

Amy turned to Russ. "If Nick and I stay here, you can come back for us," she said, bravely.

"I can make it," Nick said softly.

Amy turned to Nick. "You know how you get when you're outside too long. You can't breathe."

"I can do it," Nick told her.

"Okay," Russ announced. "So, the plan is to get back to the house, right?"

"Which way?" Amy asked.

Russ spoke with a certainty he didn't feel. "Straight ahead . . . I guess."

The kids wandered into the taller grass heading for the house. Again, they were aware of the shadows and the noises in the overgrown jungle of the grass. Suddenly, inspired by the jungle

27

surrounding them, Ron let out a Tarzan yell: "AAAHHHHHEEEEEEEEAAAHHHH!" and thumped his chest.

Everyone jumped in surprise.

"Knock it off, Ron," Russ told him.

"Hey," Ron protested, "this is supposed to be an adventure, right?"

"Will you leave me alone, Ron?" Russ asked his younger brother.

"Don't pick on me, Russ," Ron said. "You're the one who isn't even sure if we're going in the right direction."

"He has a point," Russ admitted to Amy.

Russ shinned up a thick blade of grass. From his perch on the grass stem, Russ stared into the distance. The Szalinski house loomed on the horizon. Russ slid down the blade of grass. The kids gathered around him.

"I can see the house in the distance. We can probably make it there by sunset."

"Wait a minute," Amy said. "You don't know your way around this yard. You could walk us into a ditch."

"Listen, I'm the oldest, okay?" Russ told Amy.

"You are not," Amy told him. "Besides," she drew herself up to her full height, "I am *definitely* the biggest."

"But you're a *girl*," Ron objected.

"You're *both* the oldest," Nick offered. "Why don't you both take charge?"

Amy and Russ looked carefully at one another. "Sounds good," Russ agreed with a nod.

"Well, okay," Amy said simply. But she was secretly pleased.

Just then a huge black shadow passed over the clearing where the youngsters were talking. It was a butterfly. It was so big compared to them that it blocked out the sunlight as it flew over them.

Then the sound of prolonged rolling thunder ripped through the forest of grass. The kids thought a heavy storm was brewing. In the distance, the grass blew wildly, first in one direction, then in the opposite direction. Twigs began to blow up into the air.

Nearby, a huge yellow dandelion launched itself into space. Blasts of wind from several different directions swept over the kids.

"Pretty weird," said Ron.

"Look!" cried Nick.

The adventurers raised their eyes.

A KingKong-sized power mower, roaring, shredding grass, and spewing dust as it approached, was bearing down on them at a terrifying speed.

Tommy Pervis looked the size of the Jolly Green Giant to the kids as he moved the roaring lawn mower around the lawn. Nick had hooked it up earlier with a special remote-control device. Horrified, the kids watched the machine approach. Tommy was running the mower towards them quickly and deliberately, or so it seemed. He was munching on one of his cookies from the brown paper bag that he always seemed to have with him.

Grass and twigs from the lawn mower rained and crashed around the children as they ran from the metal monster. But it was gaining on them quickly.

"Get down!" Russ yelled to his companions. "Get *down*!"

The kids dropped to the ground. Russ joined them there as they all tried to hug the earth — or crawl into it.

The loose dirt near the approaching mower was sometimes sucked in by the machine. Sometimes it was blown away from the mower in storms of flying dust, grass, and pebbles that landed like boulders.

The kids cringed.

Then the circular bottom of the mower was directly above them. They could see the giant black steel cutting-blades whirling madly just overhead. The bottom of the mower looked like the mother ship of evil invaders from an unknown planet. It hovered and threatened with its awesome size, power — and noise. The noise was deafening.

The small kids were drawn *up* from the ground by the suction of the mower. "Grab hands!" Russ shouted, taking Nick's hand into one of his and Ron's in the other. "Grab hands!" The others joined hands to form a ring on the ground.

But suddenly, Ron was torn loose from the grip of his companions.

He was sucked up towards the whirling blades of the mower!

Russ watched in horror as his brother, clinging to a branch being drawn into the machine, floated skywards in a cloud of debris and grass.

The shadow of the mower passed. A huge new trainer — the cringing kids could *smell* the new rubber and canvas of Tommy's enormous shoe — thumped to the ground near the remaining four adventurers. Then the shoe was gone too, and the noise and the danger had passed.

But what about Ron? Russ and the others wondered and feared.

What on earth had happened to Ron?

31

7

BEE DAZZLED

Russ was the first to climb out from beneath the clumps of cut grass which buried the youngsters as Tommy Pervis and the mower finally passed. Russ dashed off towards the part of the jungle where he thought he might find his brother.

"Ron! Ron!" he shouted as he ran. His companions trailed along behind him.

"Ron *has* to be in here somewhere," Russ shouted to the others as he searched through a mound of freshly cut grass.

Russ and the Szalinski kids began searching in different mounds nearby. As they worked, they called out for Ron.

After a while, the youngsters stopped and sank to the ground, exhausted from their efforts.

"Ron," Russ said softly. "Poor guy mowed down at the age of ten. . . ."

"Hey! Over here!" A voice yelled at them from the distance. It was Ron! He was hanging from the top of a bent dandelion stalk. He lost his grip on the flower and dropped from the other kids' sight. Then he bounced back into view, this time high into the air. Then Ron was bouncing up and down well above the level of the ground.

The other kids ran towards Ron and plunged into what turned out to be a patch of wild flowers growing in the back garden.

Ron was jumping on the flowers like trampolines!

He did not appear to have any control over his bounces.

"You twit," Russ put his hands on his hips and frowned as he shouted up to his brother. "You'll do *anything* to get attention."

"Hey, this is fun," Ron yelled. "Come on!"

"It's beautiful," Amy said, smiling, as she looked at the flowers all around her.

"Yeah, it's okay," Russ agreed.

"It looks like Oz," Nick added from the ground.

Ron soon discovered that the shorter flowers made the best trampolines. He bounced gleefully back and forth on top of the flowers and warbled another Tarzan yell: "AAAHHHHHEEEEEE-EEAAAHHHHH!"

"Be careful," Russ said to him warily. "You might hurt yourself." Then, almost to himself he added, "I can't believe I said that."

Ron bounced on dandelions which had gone to seed and turned into fluffy white puffballs. The tiny seed umbrellas, which seemed pretty large to them, fell on the ground around the other three youngsters like a blizzard of huge snowflakes.

Nick sneezed.

"Are you okay?" Amy asked, concern in her voice.

"It's only my hay fever," Nick said with a smile. "I'm fine." He ran to join Ron bouncing about on the flower tops. The fun was too much for Nick to miss just because of some allergy.

After a few tentative springs, Nick joined the game in earnest, leaping high up from the flower tops. "Yahooooooo!" he yelled.

A faint but persistent droning was heard in the air.

"Okay," Russ shouted. "It's time to move on now."

Nick stopped bouncing. Ron went on.

"Come on," Russ repeated more loudly.

"No way, José," Ron replied.

"I'm not kidding," Russ said. "I'm counting to five."

"Did you forget how to count all the way up to ten?" Ron teased. "He's beginning to sound a lot like Dad," Ron said to Nick.

34

"Look," Russ said impatiently. "There's something you'd both better understand. We're in a *lot* of trouble here. This isn't a game. We could die out here and no one would notice. The only way we're going to get out of this is if we all help each other."

"Right," Ron said, stopping and seeming to agree with his older brother. "But first, play-time!" He began to bounce on the flowers again.

The droning sound increased. Whatever was making the now deafening buzzing sound was getting closer.

"What's that awful noise?" Amy asked Russ as they watched the younger children play.

"Sounds like a buzz saw," Russ answered. "It's probably my Dad, working with his power tools in the garage."

"But it's coming from all different directions," Amy said in puzzlement.

"Nah," Russ replied. "It's just your ears playing tricks on you."

"Will you shut up and listen?" Amy pleaded.

The younger adventurers stopped bouncing as the source of the maddening buzzing approached and grew louder still. Amy screamed and pointed as a huge black object cast a shadow over the adventurers on the ground and over the flowers.

A honeybee hovered over the flower bed and descended towards Ron and Nick ominously.

"Hit the dirt!" Russ yelled, running towards them.

The youngsters jumped from the flowers to the ground. Ron ran in one direction, Nick in the opposite direction.

The bee landed on a flower and began extracting pollen and stuffing the sticky yellow stuff into the pollen baskets on its rear legs. To the children, the bee looked the size of a flying dumper truck.

Nick crouched beneath a flower, wheezing. The bee hovered over the flower next to Nick. Suddenly, the bee scooped Nick up and plastered him on to one of its hind legs with the sticky slabs of pollen.

Amy screamed.

"Holy . . ." Russ began.

". . . cow," Ron finished.

Nick was gasping, half smothered in pollen.

Russ sprang forward. Dashing in front of the already running Amy, he leapt on to a flower. Russ used the flower as a trampoline. Then, as the bee was beginning to take off, Russ bounced across the flower bed and leapt as high as he could go. He landed right on the back of the rising bee as it disappeared from view into the sky.

At first, Ron and Amy were frozen where they stood. "Nick! Nick!" Amy called in despair. Then she sprinted into the forest of grass. Ron trailed after her calling for Russ.

Meanwhie, Russ was enjoying a breathtaking — and scary — ride high above the garden on the back of the bee. The bee acted like an airborne bucking bronco, trying to shake Russ of its back. Russ tried to get control of it by grabbing its wildly flapping wings. But his main problem was to stop himself falling off.

Nick squirmed in the pollen on the insect's back leg. He could see Russ struggling above him on the bee's back.

"It's okay, kid," Russ called to Nick. "I'll get you out of this, somehow."

The bee flew in choppy, broken patterns, angry over the unwanted extra load on its furry back. He dive-bombed Tommy Pervis. Tommy swatted him away.

Then the bee headed in the direction of the hive.

Russ realized that if he and Nick were taken to the hive, it was all over for them. "Hold on tight," Russ yelled to Nick. "I'm going to land this thing one way or another."

With that, Russ reached down and grabbed one of the bee's wings, closed his eyes, and yanked the wing as hard as he could. Suddenly unable to control its flight, the bee spiralled straight down. The terrified boys shouted and screamed all the way to the ground which rushed up to meet them.

There was a sickening thud when the crash came. The boys were thrown free.

Russ and Nick and the bee lay motionless on the ground.

8

WATER, WATER EVERYWHERE

Nick and Russ were dazed. They sat up slowly.

Warily, they noticed that the bee was shaking and buzzing itself awake nearby as well.

The bee spotted them. It now buzzed angrily, fluttered its wings, and began to scramble across the short distance separating it from the boys.

"Are you strong enough to run?" Russ whispered urgently to Nick.

"You bet," Nick answered softly, keeping his eyes on the bee.

The boys rose together as if on signal and bolted away from the bee. The bee tried a short test flight to catch Russ and Nick.

The boys were afraid that the insect was going to succeed. They ran as hard as they could.

Then the angry bee was smacked back to the ground by a wall of water falling on it without warning from the sky.

The boys stopped and watched the now helpless bee wallow in the pool of mud.

"Are we safe?" Nick asked Russ.

"I'm not sure," Russ answered.

Suddenly, another downpour of water fell from the sky, the giant drops soaking the boys. The ground beneath their feet turned to mush. The garden around them began to fill up with water.

Russ scrambled up a blade of grass, reached back, and pulled Nick up after him.

The blade was shorter than the ones Russ had climbed previously — before Tommy Pervis had mowed the grass and *almost* mowed the kids down with it.

At the top of the blade, Russ could just see a water sprinkler. Somehow it had been turned on and was spraying water all over the place.

In a nearby part of the garden, Amy and Ron dived into a shallow cave in the ground to escape the water that had begun to fall all around them, too. A moment later they came running out again with a giant earthworm right behind them.

The two adventurers dived through the rising tide of water and scrambled away from the worm cave. They searched desperately for a safe place to escape from the deluge of water which was now forming a lake on the ground around them.

"Look!" Amy cried, pointing to something

that was shaped like a round rubber life raft. They ran for the boat.

Amy pushed and shoved Ron over the rim into the safety of the raft. But before she could climb in herself, a flood hit. She grabbed the edge of the craft and clung to its side as it was carried away by the tidal wave.

Inside the spinning raft, Ron struggled to help Amy. He took one of her hands and pulled and tugged until, finally, he got Amy over the raised rim and into the raft.

Amy lay on the floor of their small craft. Exhausted, Ron also collapsed while their boat was tossed and whirled in the raging water.

"What *is* this thing?" Ron asked, looking around inside their boat. It had a plastic-coated bottom and crimped metal sides, just high enough to keep them afloat. There was lettering along the side of the boat. Ron moved carefully and leaned over the edge so he could read the letters. It said O-R-A-N-G-E J-U-I-C-E, upside down, of course.

"Don't look now, but I think we're in a bottle top," Ron said.

Amy looked around. Ron was absolutely right. The two of them were afloat in a bottle top and they were being tossed around as if it were a *Tilt-a-Whirl*. White water rafting was okay if you were riding in a high-walled rubber raft and wearing proper life jackets, Amy thought. But rafting was quite another thing altogether in a shallow bottle top without paddles and with water coming in over the sides.

"Hey," Amy yelled. "We're taking in a lot of water!"

Nearby, Russ and Nick clung to their blade of grass. The water pushed and tugged at the boys' stem of grass and bent it nearly double, almost dumping them. Suddenly, the flood ripped the stalk of grass from its roots. It landed on its side forming a sort of canoe. Russ managed to climb into the canoe and then helped Nick struggle aboard.

The two boys were breathing a sigh of relief when a sudden surge of water sent the canoe tumbling down a small waterfall. The boat zigzagged through the perilous jungle of grass as it rode the rough water. Nick kept his eyes closed so he wouldn't have to see how close they came to crashing — and how often.

Then he heard a familiar voice.

"Russell! Nick! Help, we're sinking!"

It was Amy! Using only their cupped hands, Amy and Ron were desperately trying to bail water out of the bottle top *they* were using as a boat.

In the next instant, the grass canoe was tossed close to the bottle cap. Russ reached over to grab the side of the top. He almost tipped both of them over.

Amy stuck out her hand, trying to reach Nick, but the bottle top spun around and around, throwing her to the deck. Three more times the boats nearly touched and then were separated before the children could close the gap again.

Then, just as the bottle top seemed about to sink, a wave pushed the boats together a final time. Russ and Amy grabbed hands. Ron scrambled to the safety of the canoe, but before Amy could escape, the foundering bottle top broke away from Russ's grasp and sank out of sight into the rushing water.

The boys watched in horror as huge bubbles glugged to the surface where the other boat had been.

"Head for shore!" Russ yelled. Then as the younger boys paddled as hard as they could with their hands, Russ dived into the water after Amy. He just had to save her!

9

DOUBLE TROUBLE

At that moment, the kids heard a sweet sound, or rather a sweet silence, as the patter and splash of the huge drops of falling water suddenly stopped. The boys in the canoe bumped on to a mud bank, and tumbled out, exhausted. Nick climbed from the craft slowly and yelled for his sister.

"Amy? Amy! *Amy*!" he cried, fearing the worst.

Then, he could see Russ's head bobbing in the muddy river. He waved desperately to him and cried out again. Soon he could see that Russ had found Amy and was bringing her to shore, but she wasn't swimming by herself. Russ was pulling her.

The older boy stepped out of the river on to the soggy land, carrying Amy. He laid her carefully on the grass above the waterline. Her eyes were closed, and she was barely breathing.

"Wake up, Amy!" Nick sobbed, kneeling at her side and rocking her tenderly. "Wake up! Wake up!"

Russ held Amy gently and tried to help her breathe. She coughed, spluttering water. Her eyes blinked. She gasped and gulped air. Then she coughed again and finally began breathing normally. She opened her eyes. She was staring right into Russ's face. He blushed.

"Are you all right?" he asked.

She coughed a final time and nodded.

"Just fine," she said, sitting up, but she lay right back down again. "Well," she said, "almost fine."

That was good enough. Russ and the young boys grinned with relief, then cheered.

"Hey, brother," Ron said to Russ. "We missed you!"

Nick grinned at Russ. He was glad he'd shared an adventure with the older boy.

"You should have been on that bee!" Nick said to Ron. "It was great! And then Russ made the bee crash, and it came after us again after it woke up and —"

"We can talk later," Russ said, cutting him off. "Now, we've got to head home."

"Aww, come on, Russ," Ron said. "We're tired."

"Listen to Russell," Amy said. "We're all together again. We have to be strong. We have to

45

get home. We can't keep on wasting time here."

Ron and Nick exchanged looks.

"I bet it's almost lunchtime," Ron reminded the others.

"I bet Mum made hamburgers," Russ said. His brother nodded. Then Ron turned to Nick and Amy to explain, "Saturday is hamburger day," he said.

Thoughts of food and parents reminded the Thompson boys how strange everything had become. It made them sad to think how far they had to go — how much had to happen — before things could ever be normal again. Amy and Nick wondered if *their* mum was ever going to cook hamburgers for them again.

"Let's go," Russ said.

"Come on, troops!" Amy said.

The boys began marching behind Russ and Amy. They sang together to take their minds off their stomachs and other trouble spots.

The kids were making good progress marching through the jungle. Then Russ came to a sudden halt. Amy almost piled into him. The little boys tripped on one another, nearly falling down as well.

"Kids!" Russ said, excitedly, pointing.

"Yeahhhh!" said Amy, for there in front of

them was a cookie and it was so big, compared to themselves, that all five of them wouldn't be able to finish it, no matter *how* hungry they were.

"Wow!" said Nick. "Tommy Pervis must have dropped a whole one when the bee chased him."

"I think I've died and gone to heaven," Ron said.

"It's as big as a house," Nick remarked.

"It's got double filling!" Ron yelled excitedly.

The kids all dashed for what they saw as their lunch. But just as they were about to dig in, Ron waved his arms to stop them.

"Uh, guys?" he said looking out over their heads.

All the kids looked up. Around the sides of the mountainous cookie, they could see an army of gigantic antennae twitching.

There was no mistaking what they saw. The top of the cookie was covered with ants, and the ants were enormous!

The kids turned to run, only to find themselves facing another army of ants coming from the opposite direction. The giant ants moved closer. The kids all thought the same thing at once. "Are these ants going to feast on the cookie . . . or on us?"

47

10
ANTICS

The second column of ants was coming closer and closer. The kids were going to be trapped between the two armies.

Russ looked around for a place to hide. He spotted a leaf. "In here! Quick!" he said.

The insects swarmed over the cookie, ripping it to crumbs.

The kids watched from under the leaf.

"What pigs!" Ron whispered.

Nick started to agree with him, but sneezed instead. Ron glared at him.

"I'm allergic to —"

"I don't want to hear about it," Ron said and turned to watch the gigantic ants.

The ants continued to work on the cookie. Some of them began to carry off big chunks of it.

"That's not fair," Ron grumbled, watching the ants too. "That's was *our* cookie."

Russ gave his brother a warning look. "Stay down," he warned. "They might think we're food."

"Aah, they're only bugs," Ron said. "I squash them all the time."

"You couldn't try that now that you're as small as we are," Nick said. "Ants can lift over forty times their weight. That's like us lifting a truck," he explained.

"No kidding!" Ron said, impressed.

"How do you know all this stuff?" Russ asked him.

"I read a lot of books," Nick told him.

"You must read twenty-four hours a day!" Russ said.

Nick shrugged. "Mmmmmm. More like eight," he said. "You know, I don't think we're their kind of food."

"Do *they* know that?" Russ asked Nick suspiciously.

"Shhhhh!" Ron said, trying to quieten his companions.

While they watched in horror, an ant crept over to the leaf where they were hiding and twitched its antennae. The children huddled in the farthest corner under the leaf while the bug seemed to sniff curiously.

Nick felt a familiar tickling in his nose. He *was* allergic to ants and he *was* about to sneeze. Russ saw Nick's nose twitching. Quickly, he reached over and put his hand over Nick's face. The sneeze subsided. The adventurers breathed a sigh of relief when the ant lost interest and rejoined his army, more interested in the cookie than in a dead leaf.

Soon, the ants were nearly finished with their feast. The kids crept to the edge of their hiding place and watched. Finally, all but one of the ants were gone.

The last ant was smaller than the others. It was a baby ant, and it was struggling with a boulder-sized chunk of cookie. Every time it grasped the chunk with its big jaws and started to lug it off, the cookie piece slipped out of its grasp and tumbled to the ground.

"I say it's time for a snack," Ron said, suddenly grinning.

"Be serious," Russ told him, realizing that Ron intended to steal the chunk of cookie from the baby ant.

"I have a plan," Ron told him. With his Cub Scout Knife, he cut off a piece of grass and shaped it to look like a spear.

Russ sighed. He had learned long ago that when his brother had a plan, he was going through with it — no matter what the consequences.

"Ready, brother?" Ron asked, shaking his spear.

"I suppose so," Russ said.

The instant the ant dropped the crumb again, the boys charged it, whooping and screaming. The startled insect ran off.

"Don't let it get away!" Amy hollered. "It may bring back the others!"

That was a piece of plan Ron hadn't figured on.

"Okay, now it's time for plan number two," he said, undaunted. "Scouts to the rescue!"

While the other kids watched in astonishment, Ron ran up to the ant and jumped on its back, cowboy style. Ron clung to the ant's back while the insect ran in circles. It was a wild ride — better than anything at the carnival!

"Okay, enough fun," Russ said, watching his little brother ride the wild "pony". "Pull him over," he told him.

Ron grabbed an antenna. First he yanked to the right. Then he yanked to the left. The ant ran in circles.

"Uh-oh, I *can't* pull him over," Ron yelled.

"Some rescue," Russ told him disgustedly as they bounced along.

Amy watched while Russ and Ron tried to control the frightened ant. "Boys!" she said,

51

shaking her head in disgust. Russ tried to wrestle with the ant, but the insect shook him off easily. "Pathetic!" Amy groaned.

"I'm getting seasick!" Ron complained from the ant's back.

While the boys were fighting with the ant, Amy calmly walked over to the piece of cookie, broke off a chunk, and waited for the right moment. A few seconds later, the ant spotted her and began charging. She held her hand out in front of her so the insect could sense the cookie. The ant skidded to a stop. Ron tumbled off its back.

Slowly now, the ant approached Amy's extended hand. It seemed to sniff at the piece of cookie, then nibbled at it contentedly.

While the ant chewed the cookie, Russ walked up beside him and slipped a woven grass rope he had made around the ant's neck. The ant was captured.

"So, now that we've got him, what are we going to do with him?" Nick asked.

"Well, for one thing, if he'd let us, we could use him for transportation. He moves twice as fast as we do," Amy reasoned.

"You mean, ride him like a horse?" Ron asked.

"Sort of," Amy said, thoughtfully. "He's too small to hold all of us on his back, though."

"But he's not tame or anything," Ron said. "How will we steer him?"

"I have an idea!" Nick said. He told the others what it was.

It didn't take long to put Nick's idea into effect. The kids built a sledge out of woven grass and attached it to the ant with grass ropes like the one Ron had made for a halter. While Ron rode on the ant's back, the other children sat on the sledge.

Ron held a long stick like a fishing pole with a cookie crumb dangling from it, like bait on a hook. When the crumb was in front of the ant, he moved forwards. When Ron moved it to the right or left, the ant followed.

"Who says that junk food isn't good for you?" Ron asked. Then he turned to Amy. "Where to, Ma'am?" he asked.

"Home, James," she commanded, as if she were a fine English lady talking to her chauffeur.

"Tarzan's the name. Jungles are my game!" he told her, holding the crumb in front of the ant. With a lurch, the ant began trotting straight ahead, carrying Ron and pulling the other kids behind it on the sledge.

"Boy, I wish Dad would have thrown us out closer to the house," Nick complained to Amy.

"It could have been worse," Ron said to him.

"How?" Nick asked. It was hard for him to imagine what could have made the situation worse than being dragged across the back garden by an ant that he was probably allergic to.

"*My* dad would have tossed us down the rubbish chute!"

Nick agreed. That *would* have been worse.

11
STICKY BUSINESS

The ant pulled the kids on their sledge with Ron jiggling the cookie crumb in front of it. After a while, it walked slower and slower.

"I think our transportation system needs to have its battery recharged," Ron said.

"Me, too," Nick agreed. The ant came to a halt and the kids clambered down. They sat together in a small clearing in the lawn.

Ron looked up through the towering grass blades at the sky above them. "It's getting dark. We'll never get back in time," he said, shivering at the thought.

Amy put her arm around Ron to comfort him. "It's okay," she said thoughtfully. "At least our families will know something is wrong if we're not back by supper. They'll look for us."

"I don't think they'll see us," Russ reminded her gloomily.

"They don't even know we've shrunk!" Ron said. He felt bad enough to cry, but he would not let himself do it.

"They'll find us," Amy said. "I *know* they will."

"She's pretty gutsy," Ron whispered to his brother.

"I'm going to climb up a stalk of grass and see where we are," Russ said. He started climbing. When he was near the top, he looked up.

There, almost directly above them, Russ's father was leaning on the fence. Big Russ appeared to be watching something going on in the Szalinski back garden. He was smoking a cigarette and was about to flick some smouldering ash right on top of the kids.

Russ slid down the grass blade as fast as he could. "Look out!" he cried in warning, just in time. Flakes of ash, as big as tyres, began drifting down on them from above. As soon as they hit the still soggy ground, they sizzled. "Take cover!" Russ yelled.

The kids scattered, trying desperately to get out of the way of the ash that was raining on them. Whichever way they turned the giant glowing masses seemed to threaten them.

Ron huddled under a maple leaf — until an ember landed on *that* and burned right through it. The burning mass hung perilously above his head. He dashed away from it. Ron ran blindly

56

into the forest. He was so desperate to get away from the falling embers that he didn't look where he was going.

Before he knew it, he had skidded into a pond of brown goo. He sank in it up to his waist. It felt like quicksand — at least Ron couldn't pull himself from it — and he was surrounded by the bodies of flies who had apparently stuck and drowned in it.

"Help!" he shrieked, struggling against the mush.

The other kids ran to his rescue, zigzagging through the flying embers as they approached the sticky mess which held Ron prisoner.

"It's quicksand," Ron said to Nick in despair when Nick arrived and stood at the edge of the goo.

Nick put his hands on his hips. "That *can't* be quicksand," he said.

Ron struggled against the pull of the goo. When he finally worked one hand loose, he held it up to his face and then licked his fingers. He looked up at the others and yelled, with new desperation, "Help! Syrup!"

It was the same maple syrup he had poured on to the fence that morning to catch flies — and then thrown over the fence when his dad approached. At the time he never thought that *he* would be one of the creatures to become trapped in the stuff.

Suddenly, Ron was really terrified. The more he struggled, the deeper he sank.

"Don't move," Amy warned him. "The more you move, the harder it will be to help you."

It was all Ron could do to keep from struggling, but he could tell Amy was right. Russ reached out, trying to grab his brother's hand, but their arms just weren't long enough.

"We'll make a rope," Amy said. "We'll pull you out. Keep calm."

Ron took a deep breath and tried to believe Amy. "Hurry," he said. "Please hurry." Near him a half-dead fly continued buzzing and twitching helplessly.

Amy and the boys tried desperately to weave a rope that would be long enough and strong enough to pull Ron back to safety. They still had to dodge the glowing ash from the cigarette which showered down on them.

The kids threw a length of woven and spliced rope to Ron, but it wasn't long enough.

"More rope!" Amy commanded. They got back to work quickly.

Suddenly, there was a roaring, whooshing noise.

"What the heck was that?" Russ asked, looking up. At that second, the glowing, smouldering end of his father's spent cigarette dropped from the sky. It landed right in the syrup, still burning. The unlit end was right next to Ron, but it was clear that within a few minutes, the cigarette would burn down to that part. It was so close to him that he would burn, too!

In terror, Ron began to struggle again. He sank into the syrup up to his chest, but still managed to keep his arms free.

"We have to push it away," Amy said, studying the butt.

"Dad *promised* he'd give up smoking," Ron called to Nick.

"He *did* give up smoking," Russ told him. "In the house."

"Swell," Ron said, trying to joke about the terrible situation he was in. But there was no more joking when a piece of the burning ash fell off the butt and landed on the still struggling fly with a horrid sizzle. The fly stopped buzzing and sank into the mire forever.

"Help me!" Ron pleaded, now nearly hopeless.

To his dismay, Ron saw Nick run off. The others continued to work on the rope feverishly, but Ron was sure their fastest wouldn't be fast enough.

"Come on, boy. Come on!" Ron heard Nick urge loudly. Just then, Ron saw his young neighbour riding up on the back of the baby ant, leading it with a cookie crumb. The ant came to a halt at the edge of the goo. Nick slid off its back and tossed the cookie crumb to Ron.

"Here! Catch!" he told Ron. Ron grabbed the soggy piece of cookie and held it high.

"I get it, baby brain," he said, with a new respect for Nick *and* his brain. Then Ron turned to the ant. "Here you go, boy. Come and get it!"

The ant inched its way up a blade of grass until it bent low over the glob of goo. Its antennae twitched eagerly. Ron tried to reach for the antenna that was closest to him, but it wasn't close enough.

Then the burning cigarette butt sputtered, startling Ron so much that he dropped the cookie crumb. While all the terrified kids watched in horror, the crumb sank beneath the goo — where the ant couldn't sense it anymore or be tempted by it. The ant's antennae stopped twitching.

"Oh, no," Ron said, realizing the ant's behaviour meant that it would now lose interest in getting to him at all. He was lost in his own trap.

But that wasn't the case. The ant took three more steps on to the blade of grass. The blade dipped lower. The ant reached for Ron with its antennae. Ron grabbed for them. When he had a good grip, the ant slowly lifted his head, pulling Ron free from the syrup. Then the ant backed down the blade of grass carefully, with Ron dangling above the goo.

"I don't believe this!" Amy said, watching in awe while the ant carefully swung Ron over to safety and let him down on to solid ground.

At the same second Ron touched down, the cigarette burst into a final, deadly flame, and then smouldered and sizzled slowly.

"He saved your life!" Russ said to his brother.

"Even when you dropped the cookie piece," Nick added.

"Yeah," Ron said, shaking his head in disbelief. "He could have been wasted by the cigarette butt or stuck in the syrup same as me." Ron turned to the ant and patted him gently.

"Okay, boy," Ron told his new friend. "You're free." He loosened the grass rope from the ant's neck. "It's time for you to go back home."

"Yeah," Russ agreed. "Your parents are probably worried about you."

61

"Like ours. . . ." Nick added sadly.

In turn, all of the kids patted the ant. It stood still for the attention and even seemed to like it.

"I don't know if you can understand me," Ron said, "but from now on I'm going to be good to bugs."

"Even mosquitoes?" Nick asked.

Ron shrugged. There was no point in carrying things *too* far. "Except mosquitoes," he said.

The ant seemed to look around at all the kids. Then it turned slowly and walked off into the forest of grass.

Ron knew that he had somebody else to thank, too. He turned to Nick. "Thanks for the help, Nick," he said. "You're all right." He put his arm across Nick's shoulders.

Nick looked up at him, grinning. "No problem, Scout," he said proudly.

Ron was still covered in syrup. He walked over to a puddle of water and began trying to wash the sticky stuff off himself.

"I'm pooped," Ron said as he washed.

Nearby, Russ overheard them. "Maybe we should rest for the night," he said to Amy.

They looked up at the now dark sky. Amy nodded. "We have a lot of ground to cover tomorrow . . . I think."

62

Nick wandered off. He was following a hunch. When he found what he was looking for, he shouted for the other adventurers. They followed the sound of Nick's voice to find him.

When the other kids reached Nick, he was climbing over a huge stack of red, blue, white, and yellow building blocks.

"What are those?" Russ asked with a puzzled smile.

"My Legos," Nick proclaimed. "These are the ones that fell out of the window this morning when I closed it," Nick told the other kids. He stretched out in an upturned plastic block comfortably. "Pretty cosy," he said.

Ron climbed into a space in the block.

"Not bad," Ron said. "Better than a tent."

"Let's get some sleep now, okay?" Russ suggested. He climbed into a block. "This seems as good a place as any," he said, contentedly stretching out.

Amy settled into a nearby block, and yawned deeply.

As the moon rose over the jungle in the Szalinski back garden, the four adventurers slept.

12
DOG MATIC

When morning came, Russ sat up in his Lego bed.
He yawned, stretched, and rubbed his eyes. Then
he stood up and looked around him. By the time
they had reached the Legos the night before, it
had been too dark to see anything, but now, he
could see exactly where they were.

"I don't believe it!" he said, climbing into the
next Lego and waking up Amy.

"What?" Amy asked, sleepily. Russ pointed
over her shoulder. She turned to see her own
house — just a few yards away. They were right
next to the steps leading to the back door.

"Nick!" she shouted. "We're home! Come
on!"

"All right!" said Ron.

The children scrambled out of the Legos and
ran to the back steps of the house. There they
came to a sudden halt. For in front of them was
the first stair step. It was much higher than all five
of them stacked together.

"Uh, it's a little bigger than I thought it would

be," Russ said. He tried using a twig for a ladder, but that didn't work at all. "Don't worry," he assured the others. "I'll figure something out. We just have to come up with a plan."

Amy began to cry. They were so close to their goal, but so far from it, too. She sat down, tired of being a good sport.

"Amy, don't cry," Nick said. "Come on, even if the odds are against us, so what? People beat the odds all the time, right?"

"Sure," Russ added. "We've got *this* far."

"Yeah, we've got through a flood," Ron reminded her.

"And killer bees —" Nick said.

"And a power mower —"

"And maple syrup!"

"But how will we get inside the house?" Amy said, bringing them all back to the problem they were now facing.

Suddenly, Nick grinned. He stood up. He put two fingers in his mouth and whistled loudly.

"What *are* you doing?" Russ asked.

"Hitching a ride," Nick told him. He took a deep breath and whistled again.

In the kitchen of the Szalinski house, Quark woke up suddenly. His right ear pricked up — then his left. He cocked his head and listened carefully. When Nick whistled the second time, Quark knew it was for him.

"Quark will never hear you," Amy said.

"Sure he will. Dogs have great ears," he said. "I read about it in a book once —"

"Here, boy!" Russ yelled.

"Yo, dog!" yelled Ron.

"Here, Quark!" Amy shouted.

There was a thundering, thumping noise as Quark came bounding through the door. He was so eager to get to the kids that he tumbled down the stairs. He stood up, shook himself off, and looked around. He sniffed warily.

When he found the children who had called him, both his eyebrows popped up in surprise.

"Good boy, Quark," Nick said, patting the side of the dog's paw, as high as he could reach.

"It's okay. It's us, Quark," Amy reassured him.

"We're just littler now," Nick explained.

"Lie down, Quark," Amy said.

The dog lay down near the children, his floppy ears on the ground. They ran over to Quark's ears and used them as gangplanks to climb onto Quark.

"All aboard!" Nick hollered. The children reached the top of the dog's head.

"Phew!" Nick said, waving at the air in front of his nose. "Quark needs a bath."

There were a lot of things the kids noticed, now that they were small, that they hadn't even thought about when they were normal-sized.

"Everybody on?" Russ asked.

"Ready for take off!" Ron said.

Amy leaned over and tugged at Quark's ear, lifting it enough so that Quark could hear her little voice. "Okay, Quark," she said. "Get up. Come on, boy!" The dog stood up. "Inside, Quark. Take us to the kitchen," Amy commanded.

Quark immediately sat down and began scratching his ear — as if he thought there were fleas there.

"Cut it out, Quark!" Nick said.

The dog stopped scratching. He obediently stood up and headed for the steps. He stopped suddenly. The kids almost tumbled down, but somehow managed to grab on to the dog's fur and stay on his head. Russ looked over Quark's eyes. There, between them and the stairs, was the Thompsons' cat, Cicero — Quark's worst enemy.

"Oh, no!" Russ said, knowing that Quark was *very* scared of the cat.

In an instant, Quark spun around and began running for his life. Cicero was in hot pursuit.

"Whoaaaah!" the kids yelled, but it was no use.

Quark squeezed under the fence and dashed straight ahead — into the street! While the kids held on as tight as they could, Quark zigzagged through traffic. First he dodged an estate car, then he skittered in front of a sports car.

All around the dog, tyres screeched and people yelled. They were all angry at poor Quark.

"Look out!" Amy shrieked. A car was heading towards them very fast from the right.

"Yoweee!" Ron yelled. He saw a pick-up coming at them from the left.

Quark was so frightened he didn't know which way to move. Then he lay down in the middle of the street, directly in the path of two cars which bore down on him, and closed his eyes. The kids dived down into his fur, hoping for safety.

There was a tremendous screech of tyres and then a CRASH! The two cars hit each other head-on. They were going so fast that their front ends were lifted up off the street! Calmly, and unhurt, Quark trotted out from between the crashed vehicles, and continued on his way. Cicero was nowhere to be seen.

A few seconds later, Quark squeezed back under the fence to the safety of his own garden and trotted up the back steps of the Szalinski house.

Quark sat down quietly. The kids stood up on his head to get a good view. There, at the kitchen table were both Mr and Mrs Szalinski, sound asleep!

"They must have been so worried about us that they just fell asleep there last night," Amy reasoned. Then, "Hey, Mum's home! Nick, Mum is home. Maybe she'll stay for good!"

Nick's eyes opened wide with excitement at the thought. Then, he returned his attention to the immediate problem they faced.

Mr Szalinski's hand dangled down by his knee. Quark nudged it, trying to get his attention. Still sleeping, Mr Szalinski swatted at the dog's cold nose. Then he snored contentedly.

"Well, he may have been worried last night when he fell asleep," Nick said, "but if Quark does that again, our dad could *kill* us!"

"Let's try yelling," Russ suggested.

The kids all made as much noise they could, but the big people still couldn't hear them.

"They can't see us from here, either," Nick reasoned.

"They'd see us from the kitchen table," Ron said.

"Good idea," Amy said, nodding. "Come on, Quark! Up on the table, boy!"

First the terrier tried to reach the tabletop by stretching. He couldn't reach it that way and his efforts almost made the kids fall off him again.

"Down, Quark!" Amy commanded.

The dog seemed to understand the problem. He backed down on to the floor. Then he looked around. Nearby, there was an empty kitchen chair. He hopped up on to the chair, and from there, it was an easy reach to the tabletop. He put is front paws on the table, knocking over the sugar bowl as he did so. That didn't matter, though. When the dog put his chin on the table, the kids slid down his snout and landed safely, just inches from Amy and Nick's father's ear.

They were home!

13

THE MILKY WAY

Mr and Mrs Szalinski were still sound asleep at the kitchen table.

"It's great to see Mum at home!" Nick said, grinning.

"Oh, wow!" Amy said, hugging her brother in happiness. "She must have come home when Dad got worried about us being missing. Isn't it great?"

"It is if she stays," Nick told his sister wisely.

"*And* if we get out of this mess," Amy reminded him. Those were two big "ifs" and they both knew it. Nick sighed.

Their father continued to sleep soundly, slumped over the kitchen table. The children ran over to his ear and began yelling, trying desperately to wake him up and get his attention. He was the answer to their problem. After all, it was his amazing pulse device that had made them shrink.

"Dad! Wake up!" Amy cried.

"Come on, we're right in front of your nose!" Ron said.

"Professor!" Russ yelled.

Mr Szalinski answered the children with a honking snore.

"Dad's a heavy sleeper," Nick explained.

"Great," Ron said. It was bad news.

"If we ever wake your parents up, they'll need a neon sign to see us," Russ said to Amy.

The kids agreed that *was* a problem. "Yeah, we're so small, and this table has so much junk on it that it'll be like looking for polar bears in the snow," Ron said. "And that *only* works if you know what you're looking for!"

Nick stared at the junk on the table, including the mess Quark made when he spilled the sugar. Suddenly, his eyes lit up. "Hey, that's an idea," he said.

"What is?" Ron asked.

"Well, when explorers get lost in the snow, they make snow signs, right?"

"I guess so," Ron said.

Nick pointed to the sugar.

Ron understood immediately. "*Sugar* signs?" he asked.

"Hey, great idea!" Russ said. "And look what else is here." All the kids turned to look where Russ now pointed. There, next to the professor's chin, was a magnifying glass.

"That ought to help, too!" Ron agreed. "Lion Scouts to the rescue!"

The adventurers ran over to the mound of sugar. They began carefully rolling the giant grains of sugar into a pattern. They wanted to make an arrow which would point to the magnifying glass.

"Then, when the arrow is done, we can climb *under* the magnifying glass, so when Dad wakes up, he's absolutely positively *sure* to see us," Amy said, confidently, adding more grains of sugar to their pattern.

"Hey, we need more sugar!" Russ announced.

Nick dashed back to the glass sugar bowl lying on its side and began tossing the granules, one by one, to Ron. He passed them on to Russ, who tossed them to Amy. It was like an old-fashioned bucket brigade — and it worked! Before long, there was a distinct arrow on the table, pointing directly at the magnifying glass.

The table jolted suddenly. Mr Szalinski was waking up.

"All right!" Russ called the other kids. "Your dad's waking up — let's get to the magnifying glass!"

Before they reached it, however, there was a terrible series of resounding roars, followed by gale force winds. Wayne was sneezing. But the worst of it was that his sneezes were blowing away their sugar arrow!

"Hold on!" Russ yelled, for the kids were in danger of being blown off the table by the sneezes, too! They formed a circle and clung to one another, barely managing to stay on the tabletop. The sneezes stopped.

"Mmmmm. I'm stiff," Mrs Szalinski said, waking up and stretching.

"Me, too," Mr Szalinski agreed, pushing himself back from the table.

"Want something to eat?"

"I guess so," Mr Szalinski said unenthusiastically. He looked around as if hoping for the morning to come into focus. He saw the overturned sugar bowl. Idly, he reached for it and set it upright.

Amy, Russ, and Ron looked on in horror, for there, trapped at the bottom of the nearly empty bowl, was Nick.

"Get me out of here!" their companion called, beating at the sides of the glass bowl, but there was nothing the kids could do. "Get Dad!" Nick cried.

"The magnifying glass!" Amy reminded the others. "Let's get to it —"

The kids dashed for it. "Hurry up!" Nick urged them. Before they could reach it, though, a huge shadow fell over them as Mrs Szalinski placed a cereal bowl in front of her husband and then served him some Cornflakes from the box on the table. The cereal was going to need sugar!

Amy and the Thompson boys reached the magnifying glass and began running around under it, hoping desperately to get Mr Szalinski's attention. But his attention was focused on the breakfast in front of him. He reached for the sugar bowl and poured a generous helping on to his cereal. When the bowl got back to the table, the kids could see that Nick wasn't in it. That could mean only one thing!

Nick wasn't much of a swimmer, but he was swimming for his life, now! He grabbed hold of a piece of cereal. It was doughnut-shaped so he used it like a rubber ring. Then he realized he was in a bowl of milk.

"Help!" he shouted. "I'm allergic to milk!" But there was nothing anybody could do about it. He gagged and choked as he paddled around.

Then things turned for the worse. A gigantic spoon was thrust into the cereal bowl. Nick managed to paddle desperately away from the spoon. That time. The next time, he wasn't so lucky. Before he knew what was happening to him, he and his life preserver had a one-way ticket to the end of the line in his father's spoon.

Nick waved frantically and shouted to his dad, but nothing happened until Quark came to the rescue. The dog began barking like crazy. He was so loud and so insistent that Nick's father couldn't ignore him. Nick couldn't see what the dog was doing, but he could hear him, and he knew he was dancing around crazily.

Nick knew that his father could tell something was wrong — and Quark was trying to let him know what it was. Mr Szalinski stared at the spoon he held in his hand. Then, as Nick watched, the man's eyebrows shot up in understanding.

"Oh, my goodness!" Mr Szalinski said, spotting his son. Nick grinned and waved at his dad. Then he began pointing to the magnifying glass on the table where his sister and friends were dancing. "Oh!" his father repeated.

"What is it, dear?" Mrs Szalinski asked.

"Honey, I've shrunk the kids," he said. "They must have been accidentally shrunken by the amazing pulse device. . . ."

"*Wayne*," his wife began to protest.

"They're alive!" Mr Szalinski sputtered. "They're safe!"

He put the spoon on the table carefully. Nick clambered out of it and ran over to the others, leaving a trail of milk dripping behind him. The youngsters hugged each other with joy. They shouted greetings to the Szalinskis — though they knew they couldn't be heard. Still, they thought Mr and Mrs Szalinski understood.

Amy's mother reached for the kids. She wanted to hug her children — even though they were so tiny. Nick and Amy knew that this was one time they really didn't want their mother to hug them. She was too big, and they were so little.

"Don't touch them," Mr Szalinski, the scientist, said wisely. "They're too small to handle. You might hurt them."

"Oh," Mrs Szalinski said, disappointed.

Mr Szalinski leaned over to them and spoke quietly. "Don't worry, kids" he said to them. "You're safe now. Just wait there."

"Where does he expect us to go?" Ron asked.

"Everything is going to be all right now," Russ said, relieved that their adventure was almost over.

Mr Szalinski set a clean spoon on the table. "Can you make it on to this?" he asked the kids. They climbed on to the spoon so he could carry them carefully and safely. He picked up the utensil and then turned to head for the attic and his amazing pulse device.

"Get the Thompsons over here," he told his wife. "I'll warm up the machine."

Amy moved to the edge of the spoon and looked over. Beneath her, she could see Quark leading the way up the stairs.

"You're a hero, Quark," she said. "That was a *two*-dog-biscuit move!"

None of the kids wanted to think about what would have happened if Quark hadn't been there when Mr Szalinski actually took his second spoonful of breakfast.

Quark wagged his tailed joyously.

14

BIG FINISH

A few minutes later, Mr and Mrs Thompson joined the Szalinskis in the laboratory. Russ and Ron had waved small greetings to their horrified parents and now the kids climbed out of the bowl of the spoon — ready to be normal-sized again, at last.

"You're a maniac, Szalinski," Big Russ blustered. "Do you realize what you've done? They're ruined for life!"

"I have the atomic make-up computed," Mr Szalinski said, ignoring him. He turned to fine-tune the computer.

"If you hurt them, Szalinski, I'll personally redo your house with my bulldozer!"

"Isn't it great to know Dad's his same old self?" Ron asked Russ. Russ winked back at him.

Mr Szalinski ignored Big Russ's remarks. "Now, I have to figure the space in angstroms needed to be placed between their atoms. . . ."

"Please hurry," Mrs Thompson urged him.

Mr Szalinski reached for the on button.

"If you blow them up . . ." Big Russ said threateningly.

Mr Szalinski seemed to hear him this time.

"What's wrong?" his wife asked.

"He has a point," Mr Szalinski told her. "I haven't actually got the machine to work properly. But the kids have. What was their secret?"

On the table, in the "target area", Ron turned to Nick. "Some genius," he said.

"Give him time," Nick said calmly. "He'll figure something out." The others all hoped Nick was right.

Mr Szalinski scratched his head and looked around. He spotted the singed baseball. He picked it up and studied it. Everyone watched silently. Then his face lit up in understanding.

"The answer's been right under my nose all along!" he said.

"You like baseball?" Big Russ asked suspiciously.

Mr Szalinski ignored the question. "You see, when the two beams collided, they generated too much heat. That's why things exploded. So, somehow the baseball blocked the tracking beam and the shrinking beam worked on its own. So all *I* have to do is shut off one beam and. . . ."

He began working furiously, flipping switches

and making notes and calculations on his stack of papers. The machine sputtered to life. The beams began circling the room. Mr Szalinski tossed the baseball with his right hand as he concentrated on his job. Finally, he tossed it into the beams. Instantly, it was zapped into a miniature.

"I told you he'd figure it out!" Nick said.

"That's only half the battle," Little Russ reminded him.

The kids waited patiently.

"Now, all I have to do is reserve the polarity — and add some energy. A lot of energy, I think." He turned to his wife. "Honey, have you paid the electricity bill?" he asked.

Her face turned pale. "Just joking," he said.

The machine began to hum. Mr Szalinski leaned over it and began to cheer it on. "Come on. You can do it!" he said. "I *know* you can!"

The lights in the attic flickered. The kids looked at one another nervously and huddled together. The beams seemed to seek them out, homing in on them. The adults could see the kids' images on the computer screen. Suddenly the machine began to whine and the beams focused on Russ.

While everybody watched, Russ grew. And grew. And GREW! He jumped to the floor. Russ became five feet tall, then six, ten, fifteen feet! His shoulders bashed through the roof of the Szalinski house. His feet strained the floor to the cracking point.

Everybody except Wayne was alarmed. "A few small adjustments. Not to worry," the scientist said confidently. He bent over his machine and his stack of notes once again. His pencil flew furiously over the paper.

Little Russ looked down on his father for the first time in his life. "Am I big enough for you now, Dad?" he teased.

Big Russ was frightened. He'd always been able to bully his son, but not now! Little Russ picked up his father and held him up so they were nose to nose. Big Russ's feet dangled at Little Russ's waist!

"Uh, you were always big enough for me, son," Big Russ said. "And I'm sorry I yelled at you," he gulped. "*Really* sorry," he added. "Put me down, now, will you? Don't hurt me, huh?"

"No pain, no gain, Dad. Why don't you try pumping iron?" Russ asked gravely. Then he smiled at his father and lowered him to the floor carefully. "I'd never hurt you, Dad," he said. "I'm still the same old Russ. You see, Dad, it's not how big you are on the outside. It's how big you are on the inside that *really* counts. Size

82

doesn't matter at all."

For the first time in either of their lives, they understood that was true.

"What a kid, huh?" Big Russ said proudly to his wife.

Mr Szalinski looked up from his work and gazed up at Russ. He turned a knob on the machine. Russ became smaller and smaller until he was his normal size. He breathed a sigh of relief and stepped over to his parents. Big Russ put his arm across his son's shoulders and hugged him. His mother hugged and kissed him.

Mr Szalinski worked on the keyboard, and then pushed a final button. "Okay, now just a little *more* power — just . . ."

The lights in the attic flickered again, threatening to go out altogether. Nobody breathed. Nobody spoke.

"Come on! More juice!" Mr Szalinski said louder and louder.

There was a sudden flash of light, an explosion, and a lot of smoke. Little Russ was afraid that everything in the attic would be blown up — including the machine, Ron, Nick, and perhaps worst of all, Amy!

Before the smoke cleared, a normal kid-sized cough told Russ that things were okay. Nick was allergic to smoke.

When the fumes went away, there stood four normal-sized children.

"I knew you could do it!" Nick said, hugging his father. "You're something else!"

"You *are* something else," Mrs Szalinski said, hugging him, too. Amy joined in as well.

Mr Szalinski spoke to Nick and Amy. "I promise you, I'll never ignore you again. And if you ever, *ever* think I'm doing it . . ." he paused.

"We'll make you eat Amy's eggs," Nick suggested.

"Twirp!" Amy said.

The Szalinski family was back to normal.

The Thompson brothers looked at one another. "Hey, look!" Ron said. "I wound up taller than you!"

"You're on your toes," Russ accused him.

"Am not!"

"Are, too!"

The Thompson family was back to normal, too.

"I'm going to be famous, you know that?" Mr. Szalanski said. "I can go back to the Scientific Congress now with *proof*. I have a machine that works, and I can show it to them. They're going to love it! They're going to love *me*! This time, in fact, they're even going to love my *tie*!" He laughed, thinking about how much fun it would be when he next read his paper about his amazing pulse device.

His wife gave him another hug. Amy and Nick grinned at one another. The Szalinskis weren't just back to normal. They were better than normal.

"Hey, explorers. How about some breakfast?" Mr Szalinski invited them all.

"Yeah!" the kids agreed eagerly. After all, they hadn't had anything to eat for almost a full day.

"Pancakes and fresh maple syrup?" Mrs Szalinski suggested brightly.

"Oh, no! No syrup!" the kids chorused. The parents were more than a little surprised.

"It's a long story," Nick began.

"A *big* story," Russ said.

"No," Nick corrected him. "I think it's a teenyweenie story!"

THE BABYSITTERS CLUB

Need a babysitter? Then call the Babysitters Club. Kristy Thomas and her friends are all experienced sitters. They can tackle any job from rampaging toddlers to a pandemonium of pets. To find out all about them, read on!

BABYSITTERS LITTLE SISTER

Meet Karen Brewer, aged 6. Already known
to Babysitters fans as Kristy's little sister,
for the very first time she features in a series
of her very own.

P●INT CRiME

If you like Point Horror, you'll love Point Crime!

A murder has been committed . . . Whodunnit?
Was it the teacher, the schoolgirl, or the best friend? An
exciting new series of crime novels, with tortuous plots and
lots of suspects, designed to keep the reader guessing till
the very last page.

School for Death
Peter Beere
When the French teacher is found, drowned in the pond,
Ali and her friends are plunged into a frightening night-
mare. Murder has come to Summervale School, and
anyone could be the next victim . . .

Shoot the Teacher
David Belbin
Adam Lane, new to Beechwood Grange, finds himself
thrust into the middle of a murder investigation, when the
headteacher is found shot dead. And the shootings have
only just begun . . .

The Smoking Gun
Malcolm Rose
When David Rabin is found dead, in the school playing-
field, his sister Ros is determined to find the murderer. But
who would have killed him? And why?

Look out for:

Baa Baa Dead Sheep
Jill Bennett
Mr Lamb, resident caretaker of the *Tree Theatre*, has been
murdered, and more than one person at the theatre had
cause to hate him . . .

Avenging Angel
David Belbin
When Peter Coppola is killed in a hit-and-run accident, his
sister, Clare, sets out to find his killer . . .

Point Romance

If you like Point Horror, you'll love Point Romance!

Anyone can hear the language of love.

Are you burning with passion, and aching with desire? Then these are the books for you! Point Romance brings you passion, romance, heartache, and most of all, *love* . . .

Saturday Night
Caroline B. Cooney

Summer Dreams, Winter Love
Mary Francis Shura

The Last Great Summer
Carol Stanley

Last Dance
Caroline B. Cooney

Cradle Snatcher
Angela Creaghan

Look out for:

New Year's Eve
Caroline B. Cooney

Kiss Me Stupid
Angela Creaghan

Summer Nights
Caroline B. Cooney